T0380960

MIAUSI®

the calico cat

Story and Illustrated by Karen Castellanos Vasquez

Copyright © 2024 Karen Castellanos Vasquez.

All rights reserved. No part of this book may be used or reproduced by any means, graphic, electronic, or mechanical, including photocopying, recording, taping or by any information storage retrieval system without the written permission of the author except in the case of brief quotations embodied in critical articles and reviews.

This is a work of fiction. All of the characters, names, incidents, organizations, and dialogue in this novel are either the products of the author's imagination or are used fictitiously.

Archway Publishing books may be ordered through booksellers or by contacting:

Archway Publishing
1663 Liberty Drive
Bloomington, IN 47403
www.archwaypublishing.com
844-669-3957

Because of the dynamic nature of the Internet, any web addresses or links contained in this book may have changed since publication and may no longer be valid. The views expressed in this work are solely those of the author and do not necessarily reflect the views of the publisher, and the publisher hereby disclaims any responsibility for them.

Any people depicted in stock imagery provided by Getty Images are models, and such images are being used for illustrative purposes only.
Certain stock imagery © Getty Images.

ISBN: 978-1-6657-4451-5 (sc)
ISBN: 978-1-6657-4452-2 (hc)
ISBN: 978-1-6657-4450-8 (e)

Print information available on the last page.

Archway Publishing rev. date: 03/20/2024

Hello, I'm Miausi!

I'm a calico cat

That means I have three different colors: orange, black and white

I love to

ZZZ

sleep

eat

dance

explore
the world

Miausi's dream is to find a family. Someone who loves her and treats her well.

My dream is to find a family.
Someone I can hug at night and
whom I can feel protected with

Miausi is very curious. She loves to find new places and eat a lot of delicious food.

Wait, what's that?

9

Miausi can't resist the smell of delicious food.

What's that smell? It smells so good!

Miausi was convinced to find that smell, but she didn't know what she would really find out on her way.

PIZZERIA

Is this what it smells so good? No, this is pizza. It smells salty and cheesy

13

Miausi walked and walked until she found a park with a lot of flowers and plants.

Oh, this smells sweet and fresh!
But this is not the smell I'm looking for

15

Miausi met a lot of usual places that were not usual for cats.

This is not what I'm looking for...
But I'll make some shopping

17

Miausi bought a lot of stuff to help her to continue her way.

Fabulous and free!

Miausi decided to move faster so she took a skateboard.

Le Miau
Flower
Shop
♡

I have a good feeling about all of this

Miausi found a lot of restaurants where she experienced a lot of different odors.

Oh look at that, croissants, cookies, and macarons!

Miausi enjoyed a good meal to get energy for her adventure.

I'll grab a bite just for a minute

After a long travel, Miausi started feeling tired.

Miausi decided to take a nap in a plant pot to charge energy.

Time to sleep!

29

When Miausi woke up. She continued smelling that.

Always stretch after a
long nap to wake you up

31

Then Miausi continued walking, until she found a house where she clearly could smell the odor that attracted her.

I found it! The smell comes from that house

Miausi decided to approach the house and spied in the window.

That smell are pancakes!
My favorite food!

35

Miausi meowed all she could until the family heard her beautiful meows.

At that moment, all the family who lived in that house ran to see Miausi. So they decided to take care of her.

I'm feeling happy! I can't believe it

Miausi's new family was very happy to have her in their lives. They did everything to keep her happy and safe.

Miausi realized she found what she really wanted: a family... and pancakes.

Now I belong to a family and I'm loved

Miausi is now treated like a queen!

This is delicious!

45

Miausi is now loved and eats a lot of pancakes anytime she wants. She sleeps in her crown bed and is hugged every night.

Always loved and fabulous!

Here are some pictures

the calico cat

I want to dedicate this book to my loved ones.

Thanks to Miausi, my calico cat, the main character in this story. Miausi has been taking care of me since she arrived in my life and I can't thank her enough for bringing light and happiness to me.

Thanks to my husband Alfredo, my biggest inspiration, who has always helped me follow my dreams, I love you.

Thanks to my mom, Gaby, and my dad, Antonio, for letting me keep Miausi when she arrived and always being there for me. Thanks to my sisters Ale and Faby for helping me care for Miausi.

And thanks to my dearest friends who are always there for me, those who love me as if I were from their own family, and for accepting me for who I am, this is for you too.

Karen Castellanos Vasquez

Printed in the United States
by Baker & Taylor Publisher Services